To the little ones who love the tree children
— P.W.

To all those giving nature the care
and respect it deserves
— C.A.

PETER WOHLLEBEN

Peter and the Tree Children

ILLUSTRATED BY CALE ATKINSON

TRANSLATED BY JANE BILLINGHURST

GREYSTONE KIDS

GREYSTONE BOOKS • VANCOUVER/BERKELEY

A NOTE FOR YOU
BEFORE WE STEP INTO THE FOREST

I live in a forest in Germany, where I often tell stories to children about the animals and the trees.

Piet the squirrel is a real squirrel. Every day he scampers about in the tops of the trees growing around my forest lodge or in the meadow nearby. In winter, I put food out for him under an old pine tree, and in summer he plays with the other squirrels in the treetops.

The ancient beech trees with their children aren't far away, either. Behind my lodge, there is a preserve where the beeches can grow undisturbed. In this protected spot, no one is allowed to cut down any trees and it is always beautifully shady and cool.

I needed a special story for this book and I immediately thought of Piet. In this story, Piet is curious about families, since he doesn't have one of his own. He can't believe that even trees have families. He asks me to show him, and so we set out on our search for the tree children.

Are you ready to make the journey with Piet to find the tree children? Yes? Then I will begin the story.

We are lucky that Cale has painted absolutely wonderful pictures so you can see all the places we're going to visit. I hope you enjoy our adventure!

Every morning before Peter the forester went
out into the woods, he sat on the bench in front of his house.
He sipped his coffee, listened to the birds sing, and watched
the sun rise over the forest. One day, a squirrel scampered up
and sat down next to him as though they were old friends.
Its black eyes were brimming with tears.

"What's the matter?" asked Peter.

He wasn't expecting a reply but, to his surprise, the squirrel
said, "I'm all alone. I don't have any family."

Peter looked carefully at the squirrel. "That's hard," he said gently. "My children no longer live in the forest with me, but I still have the trees. Did you know they have families, too?"

"Really?" asked the squirrel.

Peter nodded. "Tree parents live with their children."

"I didn't know that," said the squirrel, perking up. "Can you show me these tree children?"

Peter thought. Then nodded. "I haven't seen any tree families lately. But we could look for them together."

"Yes, let's!" the squirrel exclaimed.

"Come along, then," said Peter. "By the way, I'm Peter."

The squirrel laughed. "Perfect, because I'm Piet!"
With that, he leaped off into the forest.

"Wait!" called Peter. "I can't move as fast as you."

But Piet had already disappeared
behind the nearest tree.

Peter trudged along after him, his heavy boots making the leaves rustle. All of a sudden it was really bright. They were in a clearing full of red flowers.

Piet peeked out from behind a stinging nettle where a family of caterpillars was happily munching. "Where are the tree children?" he asked.

"It's much too hot for them here in the sun," replied Peter. "We have to go deeper into the forest."

Piet ran ahead again, until . . .

"Ew!" Muddy tire tracks stretched out across the forest floor. "Can you carry me, Peter? I don't want my paws to get all dirty."

Peter nodded and Piet climbed up onto his shoulder.

They heard a rumbling in the distance. Peter followed the sound along the tracks. When they got to the end, there was a big machine busy cutting down trees.

Peter shook his head sadly. "We won't find any tree children here either. Look. The machine has packed the soil down so much that little trees can't grow in it."

Piet sighed and climbed down from Peter's shoulder.
For a long time they walked through the forest together in silence.
Until they heard a sound in the distance.

"Hup—hoa—ho!"

Piet's nose twitched. "Is that a bird?"

Peter smiled. "No, that's my friend Dana and her horse."

Branches snapped and the two of them appeared.

"Whoa, Wotan!"

The horse stopped.

"A short rest for you, my friend," said Dana, stepping out from behind the horse. She shook Peter's hand. "Who have you got there?"

Piet stood up on his hind legs. "I'm Piet, and I'm looking for the tree children."

"Ah, I see." Dana looked thoughtful. "I haven't seen any for a while."

"At least I won't have muddy paws here," said Piet.
"The horse doesn't leave deep tracks."

Peter picked up a handful of soil and
let it run through his fingers.

"Without machines, the earth stays soft and loose," he explained.

"Your trees are lucky," Piet told Dana. Then he bounded over to Peter. "Come on. We've got tree children to find!"

After a while, Peter stopped to pick wild berries for a snack.

"I prefer the seeds in pine cones," started Piet, when suddenly a big bird swooped past!

"Help! A hawk!" Piet jumped into Peter's arms.

"Hey! Off with you!" Peter shouted at the bird.

The hawk flapped its wings, releasing a shower of small feathers as it wheeled around and disappeared.

Piet peered out from Peter's arms. "Is it gone?"

"Yes, I think he's returned to his nest," said Peter.

"So even he has a family," said Piet quietly.

"Can you carry me in your jacket?" Piet whispered as he looked up into the treetops.

"Of course," said Peter.

A narrow path led steeply uphill. The trees up high
were small and twisted. Eventually the slope was bare.

"This is a lovely place, but trees can't grow where
there's no soil," said Peter.

"Oh, look at that!" Piet called and bounded
down to the clearing.

Peter's face turned bright red.

"Someone has cut down all the old trees. What an awful mess!"

"Aren't those tree children?" said Piet.

He sniffed one of the seedlings the tree planters had planted.
"They smell nice. A bit like oranges!"

"They only smell good to us," said Peter. "This smell is how trees
talk to each other, and it means that the trees don't feel so well.
They miss being shaded and protected by their families."

Piet glanced down. "The poor little trees.
This is not how I imagined it at all."

"Some trees have a hard life," said Peter sadly.
"But let's see if we can find some happy ones."

Slowly, Piet followed Peter. Finally, they arrived
in an old beech forest. The silvery-gray trees formed
a roof of leaves way up high. The forest was cool and dark.

Piet pointed to small green wings fluttering above
the ground. "Look! There are butterflies everywhere!"

Peter laughed. "No, those aren't butterflies.
Those are freshly sprouted beech children."

"I know how they got here." Piet giggled. "I hid a lot of beechnuts here last fall so that I'd have enough to eat over the winter. And then I forgot where I buried them."

Peter couldn't stop smiling. "Beech children with their parents. A beautiful forest!"

Piet bounded onto his knee. "The most beautiful forest of tree children ever. And we found it!"

The sky was beginning to turn orange.
"Time to go home," said Peter.

When they returned to the forest lodge,
Peter made himself a cup of coffee and a snack for Piet.
But Piet didn't want a snack. He hung his head.

"Piet, you're still upset . . ."

A tear rolled down the squirrel's nose.
"Everyone has a family, even the trees. Everyone but me!"

Peter set down his mug. He lifted Piet up so he could look him in the eye. "I may not be a squirrel, but I like you very much. Do you want to stay with me?"

Piet's eyes grew wide. "Does that mean we're family now?"

"Of course," said Peter.

"And we can go and visit the trees again tomorrow?" asked Piet.

"Of course," Peter said again, with a chuckle, and they sat together on the bench, watching the sun set over the forest.

MORE ABOUT TREES AND THEIR FAMILIES

1. **DID YOU KNOW THAT TREES CAN TALK?** They use the "wood wide web" to send messages through a network of fungal threads that crisscross the forest floor. They also chat by "scent mail," releasing chemicals into the air to warn other trees to defend themselves by making their leaves bitter so caterpillars won't want to eat them, or by making themselves sticky so beetles can't get inside their bark.

2. **DID YOU KNOW THAT SOME TREES STICK CLOSE TO HOME, WHILE OTHERS LIKE TO SET OFF ON THEIR OWN?** Beech children grow slowly, deep in the shade of the forest protected by their mothers. Other trees, like alders, grow up fast and alone in open spaces, preparing the land for forest trees that might want to follow.

3. **DID YOU KNOW THAT LITTLE BEECH TREES HAVE TO WAIT UNTIL A STORM TOPPLES AN ANCIENT TREE BEFORE THEY CAN GROW TALL?** When the sun shines in through the open space, the little trees grow to fill the gap.

4. **DID YOU KNOW THERE ARE DIFFERENT WAYS TO CUT DOWN TREES?** Before the invention of chain saws, two lumberjacks would stand at either end of a long saw and cut trees down by hand. Then horses would drag them out of the forest. Today, machines with long arms reach into the trees to cut them down and pile the trunks up so logging trucks can drive them away. But some people still prefer logging with horses because it is more in tune with the environment.

5. **DID YOU KNOW THAT A TREE IS AS IMPORTANT TO THE FOREST AFTER IT IS DEAD AS WHEN IT IS ALIVE?** As the wood rots away, all the nutrients it contains are returned to the forest to be used by the next generation of trees so they, too, can grow tall and strong.

Greystone Kids / Greystone Books Ltd.
greystonebooks.com

Cataloguing data available from Library and Archives Canada
ISBN 978-1-77164-457-0 (cloth)
ISBN 978-1-77164-458-7 (epub)

Editing by Kallie George
Copy editing by Antonia Banyard
Proofreading by DoEun Kwon
Jacket and interior design by Sara Gillingham Studio
Jacket illustration by Cale Atkinson
The illustrations in this book were rendered digitally.

Printed and bound in Malaysia on ancient-forest-friendly paper by Tien Wah Press

Greystone Books gratefully acknowledges the Musqueam, Squamish, and Tsleil-Waututh peoples on whose land our office is located.

Greystone Books thanks the Canada Council for the Arts, the British Columbia Arts Council,
the Province of British Columbia through the Book Publishing Tax Credit,
and the Government of Canada for supporting our publishing activities.

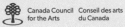